www.mascotbooks.com

CAPTAIN B

For more information, please contact:
Mascot Books
620 Herndon Parkway #320
Herndon, VA 20170
info@mascotbooks.com

Library of Congress Control Number: 2019902918

CPSIA Code: PRT0420A
ISBN-13: 978-1-68401-950-2

Printed in the United States

CAPTAIN B

Brandon
Smith

illustrated by
Rayanne Viera

Timmy was a happy boy, and today was no exception. He was woken up for school by his mother's loving kiss. He brushed his teeth and washed his face before racing downstairs to eat his favorite cereal for breakfast.

"Timmy, are you done with your cereal and ready for school?" his mom asked.

"Almost, Mom!" Timmy yelled. He ran from the table to put on his coat and meet his mom at the door.

On the way to school, Timmy loved to look out the window and listen to music. When Timmy got to school, his mother gave him a kiss like usual. She waved goodbye as he walked into the building.

When he got to the classroom, he was greeted by his teacher, Ms. Blue. Timmy said hello and raced to hang up his coat and lunchbox.

"Children, take your seats," announced Ms. Blue.

Timmy went to sit at the front of the class, but a bigger kid named Donnie pushed him out of the way. Timmy didn't like what Donnie did, but he was too scared to say anything. So he tried to forget what happened as he listened to Ms. Blue read a story.

"Okay children," Ms. Blue said.
"Please get ready for recess!"

Timmy went to recess with the other kids,
but every time he tried to play on any of the
playground equipment, Donnie got there first.

Timmy went over to the swings, but Donnie said,

"NOPE!

I'M USING THIS! "

Timmy went over to the monkey bars, but Donnie said,

"GO AWAY! I HAD THIS FIRST!"

Before he knew it, Ms. Blue called for the children to line up and go back inside. Timmy was the last one to line up.

When Timmy's mom came to pick him up from school, she noticed that he wasn't acting like his usual self. He wasn't smiling or singing, and he didn't look the least bit happy.

"What's wrong?" she asked.

Timmy didn't respond. When they got home, Timmy went right to his room and shut the door.

SLAM!!!

The next morning, Timmy's mother woke him up with a kiss just like she always did. But this morning, Timmy was unhappy.

"Mom, I don't want to go to school. Please don't make me," Timmy begged.

"Why don't you want to go to school today, honey?" she asked, surprised.

Timmy shrugged. "I don't know. I just don't want to go."

"Why not?"

Timmy hesitated. "Because we have to read in class, and I don't want to read."

"Oh, it'll be okay," Timmy's mother said. "You'll do just fine."

She gave him a big kiss on his cheek and rubbed his back reassuringly.

At school, Ms. Blue was welcoming students like she always did. When she said good morning to Timmy, he muttered "hello" under his breath and walked into class with his head down.

When Timmy went to sit down in his seat, Donnie shouted,

"CRY BABY! MOMMA'S BOY!"

The entire class started to laugh.

Timmy ran into the hallway crying. Ms. Blue had to follow Timmy into the hallway and talk to him for a few minutes before he could come back into the classroom.

For the rest of the day, Donnie made faces at Timmy and called him names whenever Ms. Blue wasn't looking.

After school, Timmy went straight to his room when he got home.

The next morning, Timmy got up way earlier than usual, still thinking about all the mean things Donnie had said to him yesterday. As he walked into the kitchen, he threw some punches in the air and thought about punching Donnie the next time he made fun of him. *That would make him stop!* Timmy thought.

Just then, the floor shook and a man landed in front of him. He had blue boots, a cape, and was HUGE!

"Who are you?"

"You can call me Captain B," the strange man said, "and I'm here to stop you from making a huge mistake! What are you doing, Timmy?"

"I'm tired of this boy bullying me at school," Timmy said. "So today I'm going to knock him out if he makes fun of me."

"Have you tried talking to him to see why he is mad at you?"

"No," Timmy said.

"Many times, people don't realize how rude they're being. They might be upset about something else, but they don't know how to deal with it. In those situations, you need to be the bigger person. Ask them why they're upset and how you can help them. Being violent won't solve anything. Take a deep breath and think," Captain B said.

Timmy took a deep breath like Captain B said and unclenched his fists. Just then, his mom called out for him to get ready for school. When Timmy turned around, Captain B was gone!

"Good morning Timmy," Ms. Blue said when he arrived at school. "Do you feel better today?"

"YUP!" Timmy said. He hung up his coat and lunch box and then saw Donnie at his cubby. Remembering what Captain B had told him that morning, Timmy took a deep breath and walked over to him.

"Hey," Timmy said.

"What do you want, momma's boy?" Donnie said.

"Why do you pick on me every day

and call me momma's boy?

It really hurts my feelings," Timmy said. "I love my momma, don't you? Why are you mad at me?"

Donnie lowered his head. "I am jealous of you," he said.

"Jealous of what?" Timmy exclaimed.

"You get to hug your momma every day, and I can't. When you came in the other day, you ran to the cubby that my mom helped me put my coat in before she went away," Donnie said.

"Well, you can have that cubby from now on, and we can be friends."

"Okay," Donnie said, wiping away his tears.

"And after school, maybe you can come to
my house and we can play!" Timmy said.

Donnie smiled. "That'd be great." He hung his coat
up and Timmy hung his up next to it. They gave each
other a hug and sat down right next to each other.

They became best friends.

When Timmy looked over his shoulder, he saw Captain B there smiling. "Great job Timmy!" said Captain B. "You had the answer within you the whole time. Remember what I told you! If you're ever feeling confused or about to make a mistake, just call on me. I'm never too far away!"

Timmy smiled.

THE
END

ABOUT THE AUTHOR

Brandon Maurice Smith was born in Philadelphia, Pennsylvania, where he grew up with his grandparents, younger sister, and mother. From an early age, he was bigger than his classmates and was bullied for his size. But, his big stature worked in his favor when he began playing football at the request of his grandfather. A person of wisdom, strength, and charisma, Brandon's grandfather was a role model to anyone who knew him. Brandon honors his grandfather by treating others with the same kindness and integrity he was known for prior to his passing. Given Brandon's own experience with bullying, he wrote *Captain B* to reach a wider audience and teach children how to treat each other with kindness and cope with difficult feelings in positive ways.